KU-348-737

THE SUN EGG

ELSA BESKOW

THE SUN EGG

Floris Books

First published in Swedish under the title
Solägget by Albert Bonniers, Stockholm, 1932
First published in English in 1980 by Ernest Benn Ltd
Published in 1993 by Floris Books
Third impression 1999
15 Harrison Gardens, Edinburgh
© 1999 BonnierCarlsen Förlag
Translation © Ernest Benn Ltd, 1980
British Library CIP Data available
ISBN 0-86315-163-9
Printed in Belgium

There was once a small elf who lived in a hollow tree in the woods. She loved dancing. In the Spring, she danced a welcome-back-sun dance; in the Autumn, a swirling-yellow-leaves dance and in the Winter, a falling-snow dance. She would dance until she was so tired that she would crawl into her tree and fall asleep.

In Summer, there was so much happening and so many interesting, funny things to watch that she didn't have so much time for dancing.

All the birds in the wood were her friends. If she saw an egg that had fallen out of its nest, lying on the moss, she would carry it up to the mother bird as quickly as she could. The birds were all very fond of her and they sang their most beautiful songs whenever she was near.

One day, when she was exploring in the wood, she saw something large, round and yellow, lying on the ground.

"What a big egg," she thought. "Where has it come from, I wonder?" She looked up and saw a bright hole in the clouds overhead.

"I know," she said. "The sun has dropped an egg and she can't see it because the cloud's in the way."

And she ran off straight away to tell her friend Larch all about it.

Larch was lying on a branch. He was always playing tricks on people and when he saw her, he threw down a fir cone and it tripped her up.

"You *are* stupid!" said the elf crossly, picking herself up. "I'll tell Crooked-Root if you do that again!" Crooked-Root was the old gnome in charge of the woods and he was the only person Larch was afraid of.

"Tell-tale!" called Larch.

"Well, maybe I won't then," said the elf. "But I shan't tell you my secret, so there!" And she ran off.

Larch jumped down from his tree and ran after her. He picked up a grass straw and a pointed stick to give her a drink of fresh birch-sap, because he wanted to make it up with her again; although really, he wasn't supposed to tap the birch trees. Crooked-Root had forbidden it.

The elf went straight to Happy Frog who lived by the lake. Happy Frog laughed at everything. She had a little restaurant which was also called *The Happy Frog.* When the elf came running up, a snail and a lizard were having lunch and Happy Frog's friend, Anxious Frog, was waiting to be served.

"What would you like—fresh bleak-roe or chopped pond-weed?" asked Happy Frog. "Or would you rather have some plantain-seed?"

"Oh, no thank you, I couldn't eat a thing. I've already had a whole wood-sorrel leaf this morning," said the elf, "but I do have some very important news. The sun has laid an egg and it's fallen into our wood. Come and look!"

Happy Frog thought this was so funny that she collapsed into giggles and almost choked. Anxious Frog had to slap her on the back.

THE HAPPY FROG
NOTICE
GUESTS ARE FORBIDDEN
TO EAT EACH OTHER
EB

The elf ran ahead to show the way and the others followed. Larch came running up with his friend, the squirrel. They were all very surprised and not a little puzzled when they saw the elf's egg.

"Just think," said the elf, " if it hatches out soon, we'll have our own sun shining here in the wood!"

"I certainly hope *not*," said the owl, peering down from his tree. "I would have to move. To-wit, to-woo."

"It'll be very hot in the middle," said Larch. "The sun has a fire inside, you know."

Just then, old Crooked-Root came hobbling up. "What's going on here?" he asked.

"It's a sun egg!" said Larch.

"To-wit, to-woo. The wood'll go up in flames soon," said the owl.

"We must stop that straight away," said Crooked-Root.

"The best thing would be if it ha-ha-ha," said Happy Frog. She meant to say that they ought to ha-tch it out in the stream, but when she thought how funny it would look, hissing under the water, she couldn't stop laughing.

"Nothing to laugh at," said Crooked-Root, crossly. "Everyone lend a hand. We'll roll the egg down to the water."

"The shell isn't even warm," said the lizard, sniffing it gingerly.

"Hurray!" shouted Larch. "It isn't a sun egg: it's a football!" and he gave it a kick.

"Don't kick my sun egg. You'll hurt the sun chick!" cried the elf.

But Crooked-Root had already seized Larch by the ear."You touch that sun egg again and you'll get what for!" he said. Suddenly, the squirrel bit off a piece of shell and scurried up a tree with it. "Ugh!" he said. "It tastes horrible!"

"Do be careful with my sun egg," cried the elf, and a chaffinch heard her and came flying up to see what was the matter.

"Listen," said the chaffinch, "that isn't a sun egg. It's a kind of sun fruit called an orange. You see hundreds of them, so I hear, in the sunny countries where some of us fly during the winter. There are as many of them as cones on a fir tree. And they have lovely yellow juice in them."

"Juice, did you say?" cried Larch, and he darted behind the yellow ball. He made a hole in the skin with his sharp-pointed stick, put in his straw and sucked. "Oh, it *is* good!" he said, and he licked his lips. "I've never tasted anything so delicious."

"What have you done?" shouted Crooked-Root angrily. Larch quickly passed his straw to the old gnome so he could have a taste, too. Then he got straws for the others, and soon they were all standing round the great ball sucking, and saying, "Oh, how lovely!" Happy Frog had less than anyone else because Larch tickled her ribs and the juice went down the wrong way. When she had finished choking, she said, "Listen, little elf; you can eat free for a whole year if you'll let me have this juice-barrel for my restaurant."

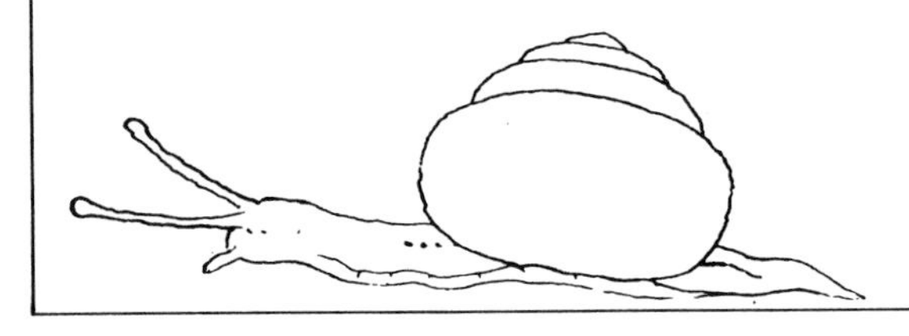

At that moment, a huge black crow came flying past, flapping his wings and cawing loudly. Everyone was scared. Suddenly, he swooped down and snatched the orange in his claws and flew off with it to his nest. The baby crows opened their beaks wide but the crow was too greedy to let them have any. He just swallowed the orange whole: but it stuck in his throat and almost choked him. Afterwards, his neck was so sore that it had to be bandaged all summer and he couldn't caw again, which rather served him right, the greedy thing.

The little elf burst into tears when she saw the crow disappearing with her orange.

"Don't cry, little elf," said the mistle-thrush. "If you like, you can come with me this autumn to the sunny, southern country where the ripe yellow oranges hang on trees. You are so light, you could easily ride on my back."

When she heard this, the elf's face lit up and she danced all through the wood singing, "I'm going to the land of the sun! I'm going to the land of the sun!"

When autumn came, the elf *did* go south with the mistle-thrush. She ran about happily in the sunshine, and soon she was nearly as good friends with the butterflies there, as she was with the ones in her own wood. Whenever she was hungry, she stuck a straw into a big orange and took a drink of fresh juice. But the lemons were much too sour, so she never drank from *them*.

So if, one day, you find an orange that is a bit dry, don't get too cross. Perhaps the elf has been drinking from it, and I'm sure you wouldn't mind if she had a sip or two of your juice.

Although the elf loved the warm southern country, she would say to the sun nearly every day, "Sun, please hurry up and shine on the woods at home, so that Spring will be there again soon."

Because when Spring came, she was going back home with the mistle-thrush. She had promised to return because the wood anemones would not come out unless she was there to dance her welcome-back-sun dance.

Crooked-Root and Larch were longing to see her. Again and again they went to see if the mistle-thrush had returned and Crooked-Root would say, "Don't be so silly, of course the mistle-thrush won't come back in the middle of winter!" But even when the snow was on the ground, he would look, too, all the same.

When at last the elf *did* come home, everyone was so pleased that they ran round her, laughing and turning somersaults.

But the whole story really began a long time before, when a small boy called Danny went looking for wild strawberries in the wood and dropped an orange out of his picnic box!